Can you believe it? I, Willimena Thomas, am a Girl Scout. But in a few days, I may have to turn in my uniform, my badges, my cute little hat, my cookie patch, and the green socks. If you think it sounds like I'm in trouble (once again), you're right. The trouble arrived in the form of sweet, innocent little peanut-butter cremes; chocolate mint; and 100 percent shortbread cookies. I sold box after box after box. I even got a patch for being the top seller in my troop. But then I ~~lost the money~~ spent the money. I was trying to do my best and live up to the Girl Scout Law, but somehow, I broke the Law at the same time. Here's how I did it, step by step.

Willie

WILLIMENA RULES!

RULE BOOK #3

How to Lose Your Cookie Money

By Valerie Wilson Wesley

Illustrated by Maryn Roos

JUMP AT THE SUN
HYPERION BOOKS FOR CHILDREN • NEW YORK

For Thembi and Nandi

Printed in the United States of America

First Edition

3 5 7 9 10 8 6 4 2

Library of Congress Cataloging-in-Publication Data on file.

ISBN 0-7868-5146-5

Visit www.hyperionbooksforchildren.com

My Rules Step by Step

Willimena's
Rules

STEP #1:
Agree to Sell Cookies

The cookie money was gone!

Well, most of it, anyway. Three weeks ago, I had $25.75. I earned it by selling Girl Scout cookies. I kept the cookie money in the purple tin where I keep my birthday money. But dollar by dollar, quarter by quarter, dime by dime, I spent twenty whole dollars of it. And not one dime of it belonged to me. Now there was only $5.75 left.

I, Willimena Thomas, was in trouble. Big trouble. The kind of trouble where

1

people look at you and just shake their heads. The kind of trouble that gets you punished for weeks.

I was supposed to give the cookie money to Mrs. Jones, our troop leader, by the last day of Girl Scouts. But I got a sore throat and couldn't go to the meeting. The next week my mom went back to work and couldn't drive me. Then my dad started graduate school, and our babysitter, Mrs. Cotton, doesn't drive. Then Mrs. Jones went out of town. Then our troop stopped meeting for the summer. Yesterday, Mrs. Jones called my mom and told her to bring the money to her house next Monday. That's a week from today.

I don't know what I'm going to do.

"Willie! Come down and get your pancakes before they get cold," my mom yelled from the kitchen.

"Okay," I yelled back. But I knew the pancakes wouldn't go down. My throat was too tight. I shoved the purple tin into my desk drawer, as far back as I could push it. I slipped on my socks, tied the laces on my sneakers, and went downstairs.

I sat down at the kitchen table across from Tina, my big sister. "Mornin', stupid," Tina said. I breathed a sigh of relief. Tina said "Mornin', stupid," almost every morning. My secret was safe.

"Tina, don't start the day calling Willie names." My mom gave Tina a warning look. Tina looked away and poured syrup on her pancakes. She drew a squiggly line with the syrup and then printed her name across her stack of pancakes. She dotted the *i* in "Tina" with a smiley face. She always does that whenever we have pancakes.

My mom poured some coffee into her cup. She took a sip, looked at the clock, and gasped. "Oh, my! Look at the time!" she said.

My mom works at a newspaper. She's always in a rush. The good thing about her working at the paper is that we always know what's going to be on the front page. The bad thing is: Mrs. Cotton, our babysitter.

Mom kissed me and Tina before she headed out the door. "Tell Mrs. Cotton that there's tuna fish for lunch, and tell your dad to buy some food for Doofus Doolittle," she said.

Doofus Doolittle is our cat. His fur is black, and he has a pointed face and big golden eyes. He's the cutest cat I've ever seen.

I spread some butter on my pancakes, picked up the syrup bottle, and held it over my pancakes. Ten dinky drops dripped out. I glared at Tina. She picked up a forkful of pancakes and nibbled on them. Syrup dripped off her fork onto her plate.

"Pig!" I said. Just my luck, my dad was coming down the stairs and heard me.

"Willimena!" Dad wrinkled up his face into a frown. "I don't want to hear any name-calling this morning."

"But she called me stupid, and you told her not to call me that anymore," I said. Tina rolled her eyes.

"Tina!" He still had a frown on his face. "I've told you about that. I don't want to hear you say that word again." He poured some water into a kettle to make himself a cup of peppermint tea.

"But she always says mean things to me," Tina said.

"Tina, you're my big girl. You should know better. It's up to you to set a good example," my dad said.

"But that's not fair! She always gets away with everything just because she's younger than me." Tina banged her fork down on her plate with a frown.

"No, I don't!"

"Yes, you do!"

"You two!" My dad shook his head. "I want you both to stop right now."

Doofus Doolittle came over and rubbed

against my dad's leg, and he bent down to
pat him.

"Morning, Mr. D.," he said to our cat.

"Mom said not to forget to buy Doofus
some food. He's almost out," Tina said.

"Thanks for reminding me, Big Girl," my dad said.

Soon there was a knock at our kitchen door and my dad answered it. Tina rolled her eyes, and I poked out my mouth. We knew who it was. It was Mrs. Cotton. The one thing Tina and I agree on is Mrs. Cotton.

"Good morning, Mrs. Cotton," my dad said.

"Good morning, Mr. Thomas and little Thomases," Mrs. Cotton said. Every morning she says the same thing. It gets on my nerves.

"Good morning, Mrs. Cotton," Tina and I said together.

My dad finished his last sip of tea. "Well, it's time for me to go," he said. "Now, I want you two to behave yourselves."

"We will," we both said.

But then I remembered there was no syrup left. "Dad, can you get some syrup off the shelf before you leave?" It was on the top shelf of the pantry, and I knew that Mrs. Cotton wouldn't climb up on a stool to get it.

"Sure, sugar," my dad said. He moved around some cans and jars, then put some on the counter. He stood on his toes and felt the back of the shelf with his hand. He shook his head. "I don't think we have any more, Willie. I guess you'll have to have honey," he said. He took down a jar of honey with a smiling bee on the label and put it on the table in front of me. I don't like honey on pancakes. They don't taste the same. I threw Tina a mean look.

"You hogged all the syrup!" I said.

"Early bird gets the worm," Tina said. She took another bite of her pancakes.

"But that's unfair!" I wailed. "You can be so mean, Tina! I'm going to get you back for this," I said. I felt like I was going to cry.

"'I'm going to get you back for this,'" Tina said. She was imitating me. The only thing that makes me madder than when Tina calls me a crybaby is when she imitates me.

"No more, girls! Stop this right now!" my dad said. This time we knew he meant it.

"Tsk, tsk, tsk," Mrs. Cotton said and shook her finger at us. "Little Thomases, you *must* act like nice little ladies! You must behave."

I spread some honey on my pancakes.

It was so thick it tore a hole through the top pancake. I took a bite. I gave Tina the hardest kick I could under the table. I knew it was a terrible thing to do, but I did it anyway.

"Ouch!" Tina screamed.

"Got you back!" I whispered. I pulled my chair out of reach of her foot. Tina narrowed her eyes and glared at me.

"Dad," she said as my father opened the door to leave.

"Yeah, Big Girl?"

"Did Mom tell you that Mrs. Jones called?"

The pancake with the honey stuck to the top of my mouth.

"What did she want?"

"She wants you or Mom to bring over Willie's cookie money next Monday. All twenty-five dollars and seventy-five cents of it."

I took a big gulp of orange juice.

"Then one of us will take it to her," my dad said.

"All twenty-five dollars and seventy-five cents?" Tina asked.

"Sure. Is that how much money you earned, Willie?"

I couldn't say anything. I couldn't even look my dad in the eye. I felt worse than I had ever felt in my life.

STEP #2:
Sell More Cookies than Anyone Else

You probably think my big sister Tina runs a close second to the meanest monster in my scariest nightmares. But Tina is nice most of the time. Well, some of the time. Okay, maybe a couple of days a month.

When I told Amber, who lives next door, everything that had happened, she shook her head. Amber is my best friend. She has an older sister named Lydia, who is the same age as Tina.

"That's bad news, Willie, real bad news,"

Amber said. We were sitting on her back porch playing checkers, which is our favorite game. We play it every day. Amber jumped one of my pieces and moved to the king's row. "Do you think Tina knows the money is gone?"

"Maybe. She was probably snooping around my things like she always does," I said. I got mad just thinking about it. I double jumped Amber. "Crown me!" I said. It was the best thing that had happened to me so far that day.

"Good move!" Amber said, then plopped a checker on top of mine. "If I were a big sister, I'd never be mean the way Lydia and Tina are to us," she said.

"But sometimes Tina is nice," I said after a while. "If it hadn't been for Tina, I wouldn't have made any money at all."

"You're right about that," Amber said as she moved a piece and then took it back. Tina, my sometimes-mean big sister, had helped me become a super salesgirl.

I had been really scared the day that Mrs.

Jones told our troop we were going to sell Girl Scout cookies. I didn't think anybody would buy them from me. I was afraid that I would ring the doorbell and nobody would answer. I was scared I wouldn't know what to say. I was sure I'd be the only Girl Scout in the troop who wouldn't sell any cookies.

But Tina had come to the rescue. She told me what to say. She even stood at my side when I made my first sale.

Every night after we took our baths and brushed our teeth, Tina and I would rehearse. "Smile, Willie. Always smile," Tina said. "No matter how mean somebody acts, smile. Pretend you're doing a commercial on TV. Let's try it again." Then Tina would get into the closet and close the door behind her. I'd knock, and she would pretend to be a mean customer.

"Can I help you, little girl?" she would ask in a gruff voice.

We rehearsed about five times that first night, until my mom told us to go to bed. After two or three nights of rehearsal, Tina decided that I was ready to sell my first box of cookies, and she was there to help me out.

"Ring the doorbell. And whatever you do, don't just stand there looking dumb!" she said. "And remember what I told you about smiling. If you forget, I'm going to kick you on the ankle!"

But I didn't forget. Tina told me to start out with somebody easy. I chose Mrs. Ross. She is the nicest lady on our street. Mrs. Ross bought three boxes of cookies. I was on my way. By the time it got dark, I'd worked my way up to Mrs. Pyle. Everybody on our street calls her Pyle the Pill. Mrs. Pyle never smiles. She always yells at us when we play in front of her house. But Mrs. Pyle bought two boxes of cookies. I couldn't believe it!

The next day, Tina and I crossed Chestnut Avenue, and I sold cookies over there. I had so many cookie orders I could barely write them all down. I was a super salesgirl! The next week was even better than the first. By the end of the week I'd made sixty dollars. I took it to my troop meeting and turned it in. Mrs. Jones said that I had sold more cookies than anybody else. And it had all been because of Tina. The third week, I earned $25.75.

That was when my troubles began.

"Sometimes big sisters will look out for you when nobody else will," Amber said as she jumped me again.

Then she said what I feared the most. "You never told me what happened to the money, Willie. Twenty dollars doesn't just disappear."

"I-I-I spent it," I said, my voice quaking.

"You spent it? On what?" Amber asked.

But before I could say anything, Lana and Lena, the twins who live at the other end of our street, ran up on the porch.

Amber didn't know it, but the answer to her question had just plopped down next to her.

RULE #3:
Find a Very Worthy Cause

Lena and Lana look exactly alike. They wear the same kind of sneakers—red and white with blue shoestrings. They both have teeth missing in the same spot. They talk the same way—very fast.

Lena and Lana have lived on our street for only about three weeks, with their aunt, Miss Wynn. But I feel like I've known them forever. They're new kids, but they don't act that way. Before they came, Miss Wynn lived by herself. Her house is very old. The shutters on the windows are loose and hang to the side. The grass in the front yard is very long. Before Lena and Lana moved in, Tina and Lydia used to tell me and Amber that her house was haunted. We believed them. A lot of kids on our street wouldn't ring Miss Wynn's bell on Halloween.

But that's all changed now. Everybody knows the house is okay because Lena and Lana live there.

The funny thing about Lena and Lana is that one always knows what the other one is going to say. One of them says something, and the other one finishes her sentence for her. They are funny when they really get going. Amber and I could listen to them for hours. They started in right away when they joined us on the porch.

"Did you get the key from—" started Lana.

"Aunt Wynn gave it to—" finished Lena.

"Don't say—" said Lana.

"But she left it with—" started Lena.

"But that was last—"

"Don't say Thursday because—"

"Well, you had it last—" said Lana.

"No, you—"

Lana and Lena argued back and forth, beginning and finishing each other's sentences for the next five minutes.

"So who has the key?" Amber asked them.

"Nobody!" Lena and Lana said together. "We're locked out again."

We all laughed.

"That's bad news, real bad news!" said Amber.

"So why doesn't your aunt leave the key in a secret place?" I asked.

Lena and Lana shrugged, moving their shoulders in the very same way.

"So what are you going to do for lunch?" It was close to lunchtime, and I was starting to get hungry. Lana and Lena looked at each other and shrugged. The expressions on both their faces told me the answer.

Just then, Mrs. Cotton came walking down the street.

"Willie, Willie, Willie!" she called out. She spotted me sitting on Amber's porch, and she came over to us.

"Thank goodness, I found one little Thomas. Where is the other little Thomas?"

"In her room," I said, "where she's been all day." I didn't mean to sound fresh, but that "little Thomas" business was bad enough at home. I couldn't stand it out here where everybody could hear it.

"Well, it's time you came home too. It's almost time for lunch," Mrs. Cotton said, and then turned to go.

I got up to leave. Lena and Lana both sighed together.

"Would you like to come to my house and have lunch?" I asked them.

"Sure, Willie, thanks!" they said together.

We said good-bye to Amber and headed back to my house to get something to eat.

The three of us came into my kitchen and sat down at the table. There were two tuna-fish sandwich halves left on a plate. They had been made with the ends of the loaf. One slice was white, the other was brown. Neither had a crust. Tuna fish spilled from the sides of both.

Tina had already taken the two good halves and was munching away. The ketchup bottle was next to her juice. Tina liked ketchup on her tuna-fish sandwich. She put huge dots of ketchup on her plate.

Then she dipped the end of her sandwich into the ketchup. Then she ate it. Tina is probably the only person in the world who likes ketchup and tuna fish. I picked up one of the ugly sandwiches. I watched Tina eat her tuna-and-ketchup sandwich. I put my sandwich back on the plate. I didn't feel like eating.

"Can I—?" Lana asked me.

"Have your sandwich?" added Lena.

"I asked first," Lana said.

"We'll share!" said Lena.

Lena and Lana shared one half of the sandwich that was left and quickly ate it. I knew they must really be hungry. Anyone who could eat an ugly sandwich like that, sitting across from Tina and her ketchup-and-tuna-fish feast, had to be.

"Want the other one?" I asked.

"Sure!" they said together. "Thanks, Willie!"

That was when Mrs. Cotton came into the kitchen.

"Please put that sandwich back!" she said to Lena. We all turned around to

look at her in surprise. Even Tina put down the ketchup bottle. "Young lady, please put that down. That last sandwich belongs to Willimena," Mrs. Cotton said.

"But I don't want it!" I said. "I want Lena and Lana to have it."

"Mrs. Thomas made those sandwiches for the little Thomases, not for other children. Please put it back," Mrs. Cotton said. Lena put the sandwich back on the plate. Lana looked at the floor. I felt terrible.

"That's not fair," I said to Mrs. Cotton. I was mad now, too. But it didn't seem to matter.

"Children must eat in their own homes," she said.

"We'll go," said Lana quietly.

"But where will you go?" I asked.

"Home," Lena said. I wondered if she had forgotten that they had lost their key. I could tell Lena felt like crying. I thought about telling Mrs. Cotton what I knew. But I knew Lena and Lana probably wouldn't want me to, so I kept quiet.

Lena looked at Mrs. Cotton. "My aunt left some—"

"Peanut butter for us," Lana finished her sentence.

I knew they weren't telling the truth. But I didn't say anything. I just watched them go out the back door. Mrs. Cotton began to clean up the dishes.

"Eat your sandwich, Willimena," she said.

"No!" I said.

She looked at me and then she sighed. "Suit yourself," she said, and went back to her cleaning.

I began to think again about the secret Lena and Lana had told me at school when they first moved to our street. . . .

"If we tell you something, do you promise not to tell?" Lana had said.

31

"Sure, I won't tell anybody," I said.

"You promise?" Lena said.

"I promise," I said. I wondered what it could be.

"Our mom is real sick," Lana said. "We're living with Aunt Wynn until she gets better."

"Aunt Wynn works nights," said Lena.

"And sometimes days," Lana said.

"She doesn't have a lot of money. And sometimes we don't have enough money for lunch," Lena added.

"Don't you get hungry?" I'd asked. They looked at the ground and then at each other and then away.

"Sometimes," Lana had said.

Because of mean old Mrs. Cotton, I knew they must be hungry now. I wondered what I should do.

I decided to go and look for Lena and Lana, but couldn't find them. I got hungry after about an hour and went inside to make myself a peanut-butter-and-jelly sandwich. But when I started to eat it, I started to think about Lena and Lana. I put down my sandwich and wondered if they'd finally gotten something more to eat.

RULE #4:
Make a Donation:
The Cookie Money??!!

If you haven't guessed already, I'll tell you what happened to the cookie money. I spent it on Lana and Lena. After they told me how they didn't have enough money for lunch, I bought it for them. I didn't tell them where I got the money.

I bought them lunch every day for a week and a half. Each day, we'd go to the cafeteria and I would buy them spaghetti or fish sticks or hamburgers, and ice cream for dessert. On the way home, we would stop at the pizzeria and I would buy slices of pizza for them to take home. The first day, it was hard to spend the money because I knew it wasn't mine. But each day, I saw how happy Lena and Lana were. But each night, I couldn't sleep because I knew it was wrong. Every day I wanted to tell Mom and Dad—but each time I chickened out. I promised Lena and Lana I wouldn't tell anybody.

I was still worried about Lena and Lana that night after Mrs. Cotton made them go home. I couldn't go to sleep. I was wondering where they had gone. Maybe they'd found the key or called their aunt. Then I began to think about the cookie money. It was Monday night. If I didn't find a way to put it back, in six days everybody would know that I had spent it.

What was I going to do?

I tried to think of an excuse to tell Mrs. Jones. Maybe I could tell her that somebody had stolen the money. But my parents would know that wasn't the truth. And what's worse, I'd know it, too. Maybe I could say that I lost the money. Or, should I just tell Mrs. Jones the truth? I wondered.

I started to imagine about what people would say if I told the truth. Everybody would know what I had done, that I spent money that didn't belong to me. I would probably end up getting kicked out of Girl Scouts. I'd never heard of anybody getting kicked out of Girl Scouts. It was probably one of the worst things that could happen to a kid—like getting kicked out of nursery school. It was the kind of thing nobody would forget. I tossed and turned some more.

"Go to sleep, Willie. You're keeping me awake," Tina said. Her bed is on the other side of the room, but I guess she could hear me moving around.

"I can't."

"Count fish," Tina said.

I tried. I'm usually asleep before the tenth fish jumps and dives.

But tonight it didn't work. The fish made me think about fish-and-chips—one of my favorite meals. That made me think about Lena and Lana again. I wondered what they had had for dinner. That made me remember the cookie money and how $5.75 was all that was left. I started to worry again about what I would say when my mom asked me to get it on Monday. Then my pillow fell on the floor. When I reached down to get it, I knocked the lamp off the table near my bed.

"What in the world is wrong with you?" Tina yelled.

"I've got a lot of things on my mind," I said as I got back into bed.

"Like what?"

"Did you think that Mrs. Cotton was mean to Lena and Lana today?" I asked.

"Yeah! She's always being mean to somebody," Tina said.

"Did you know that Lena and Lana don't get enough to eat?"

Tina didn't say anything. I thought maybe she was asleep, but then she said, "Really?"

"You know how every day after you and

I get lunch, Lena and Lana get dessert?"

"Yeah. That's really cool!" Tina said.

"Remember how last week they came to school with that big turkey-and-cheese submarine, and they ate half, and then wrapped it up and took it home?"

"Yeah. Their aunt must be the bomb, giving them all that money to spend on food," Tina said.

"They didn't get the money from their aunt," I said.

"Then where did they get it?"

"Th—th—they got it from me," I said.

Tina sat up in bed. "From you, Willie! Where did you get it?"

"I—I gave them the cookie money." I couldn't believe it, but I said it.

It was out.

Tina gasped. Even in the dark, I could

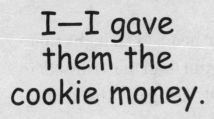

see her shaking her head. "I thought there was some reason you had not turned in your cookie money! You gave them all of it? Why?"

"I told you. Because they were hungry, and I wanted to help," I said. "But, I only gave them twenty dollars of it."

Tina didn't say anything for a very long while. There was no noise at all in our room. I thought she had gone to sleep. But then she sat up again.

"Whew . . . that's a drag, Willie."

"I know," I said.

"Big trouble," she said.

"I know. No TV," I said.

"No TV for a long time!" Tina replied just a little too quickly. "So, what are you going to do when Monday comes?" she asked.

"I don't know, Tina. I just don't know!"

Then I did something that I hate to do more than anything in the world, especially in front of Tina. . . .

I cried.

I cried for Lena and Lana and because their mother was sick.

I cried because I hated how mean Mrs. Cotton had been to them.

And I cried because I had spent the cookie money and let everybody down.

Then Tina did something that made me forgive her for all the mean stuff she'd ever done to me. She came and sat down on my bed. She put her arms around me and held me very tight.

"Don't worry, Willie. I'll come up with a plan," she said.

"What kind of a plan, Tina?"

"I don't know yet. It will have to be something where we can make money fast. By next Monday."

"But what, Tina? What?"

"Have I ever let you down before?"

I could think of at least five times when she had, but I didn't say it.

"Don't worry, Willie. Now go to sleep," she said.

And I did.

STEP #5:
Make the $$$ Back!

The next morning I asked Tina about her plan.

"End of the day, Willie. End of the day," she said. "I'll tell you at the meeting when I tell everybody else."

"Meeting? Why can't you tell me now?" I wanted to know. But Tina just smiled.

After lunch, Tina and I went outside to play. Our house is on the end of the block. Amber and Lydia live next door to us. Next to them live Betty and Booker.

Betty is eight. Booker is four. The

Greenes live next to Betty and Booker. There are so many people in the Greene family, it's hard to count them all. Once, I thought that there were only five. But then two cousins moved in from Detroit. Now there are seven. They all have round faces and big teeth, even the cousins, and they all have the same laugh. They also all have names that begin with G.

Next to the Greenes lives Mrs. Pyle. Mrs. Pyle lives by herself. She always complains when the Greenes' soccer ball rolls into her yard. She also complains about the noise when we all play in the Greenes' backyard, which is almost every day. She doesn't like animals much, either. Each of the Greene children has a pet, and Mrs. Pyle complains about the pets.

Pauline lives next to Mrs. Pyle. Besides

Amber, Pauline is my best friend on the street. She has a great babysitter named Candy, who is a really cool teenager.

Pauline is the only kid on the block who has ever been inside Mrs. Pyle's house. She says that Mrs. Pyle has a cute little canary named Tweetie. She's the only kid who has ever seen him.

Lena and Lana live in the last house. Now every house on our side of the street is filled with kids, except Mrs. Pyle's.

Almost every other day, somebody on our street will call a block meeting. Then we all meet in the Greenes' back-yard, because it's the biggest. Tina called a meeting today, and the word spread quickly.

The Greenes' house is big and about a hundred years old. It used to be a school,

and the backyard used to be the playground.

At the end of the Greenes' long back-yard is a merry-go-round. It's the best thing on the block. When it's whirling fast, it's the greatest feeling in the world.

But today, when it was time for the block meeting, nobody rode on the merry-

A kid I know lost some money that didn't belong to her.

go-round. Everybody just sat on the ground and listened to what Tina had to say.

When the meeting was ready to start, Tina cleared her throat.

Everybody got quiet.

"A kid I know lost some money that didn't belong to her. If she doesn't get it back by Monday she could go to jail," Tina said.

"That's dumb! They don't put kids in jail!" George Greene said.

Jail! I had never thought of jail! I hope George knew what he was talking about. Suddenly, I pictured myself behind bars, eating pancakes with no syrup or honey. Just cold, dry, stick-in-the-throat pancakes, with only water to wash them down.

"Who lost the money?" I faintly heard Gregory Greene ask.

"Someone everybody knows," said Tina.

"How did she lose it?" asked Gregory.

"None of your business. But I have a plan to make the money back. I need everybody's help."

"We'll help," Gregory said after a minute. "What's your plan?"

Tina smiled. "Lemonade! Willie and I are going to have a lemonade sale to help the person who lost her money get it back. We want everybody to say that they will buy some."

"That's the dumbest idea I ever heard," said George Greene.

"Tina! Is that the big plan you've been thinking of all day? What kind of plan is that?" I yelled out. I couldn't believe what Tina had just said.

"Nobody sells lemonade anymore!" said Candy, who was watching Pauline.

"Plus, who's going to buy lemonade from kids on the street when they can get it at home?" asked George.

"It will work," Tina said with a smile.

"Maybe it will," said Amber.

"We said we'd help, so we will," said

Gregory quietly. "Tina and . . . her friend . . . need help. It's the spirit of the block to help out people who live here."

At that moment, I thought Gregory was the smartest, kindest kid I'd ever known in my life.

"Are you sure it's going to work, Tina?" I asked her that night before we went to sleep.

"Don't worry, Willie," Tina said. "Don't I always keep my word?"

I bit my tongue really hard. Sometimes it's best to keep your thoughts to yourself.

STEP #6:
Plan A: Remember, It Takes Money to Make Money

The next morning started out like any other. My mom called me and Tina down for breakfast. We drank our juice and ate our cereal. My mom left for work. My dad left for school. Mrs. Cotton called us little Thomases. Everything was the same. Except that it was Wednesday. There were five more days until the cookie money was due.

Before we went outside, Tina wrote down the things we needed to have to make the lemonade sale a success: lemons, cups, and sugar. Then she read the list aloud.

"You need something to make the lemonade in," I suggested.

"Like a pan or a pot or something," she said, agreeing. Then she added *big pot*. "Done! Now we have to buy all the ingredients."

"What do we have to buy?"

"Sugar and lemons, of course," she said.

"How are we going to buy them? We don't have any money."

Tina looked at me, then smiled. It was the smile she wore when she knew something I didn't. "It takes money to make money," Tina said. "You'll have to spend some of the money you have left."

She was talking about the five dollars

and seventy-five cents that was left from the cookie money.

"No!" I said.

"How else are we going to buy the lemons and sugar?" she asked.

"We have instant lemonade leftover from last summer," I said, even though I knew that wouldn't work. "Or we can take the sugar from the sugar bowl and use the lemon juice in the refrigerator."

"Nobody will buy lemonade made from bottled lemon juice. We have to make it from scratch. You can't use a mix. We have to use real lemons and lots of sugar," Tina said.

"Then we can borrow the lemons from Amber's mother," I said. Amber's mother likes to make pies, cookies, and cakes. She always has stuff like lemons. "We can borrow the sugar, too."

"Get the money, Willie," Tina said impatiently.

I went into the purple tin in the drawer in our bedroom. V-e-r-y s-l-o-w-l-y I got out the last of the money, all $5.75.

I gave the money to Tina. Now the cookie money was completely gone. The purple tin was empty. All $25.75 had been spent. Now I was certain I was going to jail.

Tina asked Mrs. Cotton if we could go to the corner. She said that we could as long as we didn't cross the main street.

"Somebody making lemonade?" said Mr. Curtis, the owner of Curtis's Fine Groceries, the store at the corner.

"We're going to sell it," Tina said.

I couldn't speak.

"Great idea!" Mr. Curtis said. He wiped

his forehead. "It's a great day for a lemonade sale!"

Tina grinned. Maybe her plan would work after all.

Tina bought eight lemons, which came to $2.00. She bought five pounds of sugar for $2.00 and three dozen small paper cups for $1.75.

The cookie money was completely gone now.

I tried not to think about it.

When we came back from the store, we went to Amber and Lydia's house to drop off everything we'd bought. Mrs. Washington, Amber and Lydia's mother, gave us permission to use her kitchen and one of her big pots if we promised to clean up.

We decided that the sale would be at 1:30 P.M., after everybody came back from lunch. We decided to sell the lemonade for seventy-five cents a cup. We knew it was a lot of money, but Tina said we'd call it the "Best Lemonade in the World." We hoped that people would believe it.

Then Tina and Lydia read off everyone's chores. She and Lydia decided that they would make the lemonade, and that Amber and I would make the signs and hang them all around the street.

Amber and I got some typing paper from Mrs. Washington and carefully printed the signs. They all said the same thing:

Best Lemonade in the World
75¢ a Cup

When Amber and I finished making the signs, Tina and Lydia let us help with the lemonade. First, we all washed our hands carefully. Amber and I washed the lemons. Lydia and Tina got a cutting board, and Mrs. Washington helped them cut the lemons in half. Then they squeezed the lemons into a bowl and poured it into the pot. Lydia added water. Tina poured in sugar. Then she tasted it. She added some more sugar. Then she tasted it again, and poured in some more.

Mrs. Washington helped them put the pot into the refrigerator so that it would get cold. Then Amber and I hung the signs.

After lunch, we got a table from the Greenes' backyard and set it up in front of Lena and Lana's house. We were ready to go.

Gregory Greene was the first customer. "Here's my money," he said.

I took his seventy-five cents and put it into the purple tin box. Soon there was a line of kids from our street and one or two new kids from another. Then the mailman joined the line. A man who was delivering packages got in line, and Candy, Pauline's babysitter, got in line, too. Even Mrs. Cotton came out and got in line. Maybe Mr. Curtis was right, and people would buy lemonade because it was a hot day.

"I'll take two," said Mrs. Washington. She gave us one dollar and fifty cents.

"Give us two," Lena and Lana said. I wondered where they had gotten the money, but I didn't ask. I was too happy to get it.

"I'll take three. One for me and two for

my parents when they get home from work," said Pauline.

"Great!" I said as I poured her three cups.

"I'll take two, too. Just to help out," said Candy.

In ten minutes, we had made ten dollars. Things were looking up. Then George Greene held out his seventy-five cents.

"One," he said, and I gave him a cup. He dropped his seventy-five cents into the can. He took a sip. Then he spit it out.

"Yuck!" he said. "This junk stinks! It's terrible!" He bent over and grabbed his stomach as if he were going to throw up.

I looked around at the other customers. Everyone was talking quietly. Some people had poured their lemonade out on the ground. Some had poured it on bushes.

Most people had poured it in the gutter.

Nobody was drinking it. The kids who had been in line behind George stepped out of line.

"False advertising! False advertising!" George Greene yelled. "This isn't the best lemonade in the world. This is the *worst* lemonade in the world!"

Several kids started to laugh. I looked at Amber. She wouldn't look me in the eye. Lena and Lana started to giggle.

I poured a cup for myself.

George was right. It tasted horrible. It tasted just like sugar and water. I couldn't taste any lemons at all.

"Tina! Taste the lemonade," I whispered.

Tina stopped pouring a cup and gulped it down quickly.

"Tastes all right to me," she said.

"No, it doesn't," I whispered again.

"It tastes good, Willie." She drank another cup.

Suddenly, I understood the miserable truth. How would someone who liked ketchup on tuna fish know how good lemonade would taste?

"I want my money back!" yelled George Greene.

"Sorry!" said Tina. "You paid for it. There's nothing wrong with the lemonade."

"Give me my seventy-five cents back!" yelled George.

"No!" Tina yelled back.

"Give it back!" said George again. He was as determined as Tina.

"No," Tina said.

I don't like to think about what happened next. George tried to get his money out of my tin box. Tina tried to stop him. George shoved Tina out of the way. Tina shoved him back. George fell into the table and knocked over the lemonade stand. The lemonade pot tipped over. Lemonade was everywhere! It fell on George and Tina. It dripped down the side of the Greenes' old table and onto the sidewalk. It flowed in front of Lena and Lana's house and down the street toward Pauline's like a river.

"You're disgusting, George Greene!" Tina screamed. "Look what you made me do!"

Mrs. Greene came running outside to see what had happened.

"What a mess! George, did you have something to do with this?" she asked.

George dropped his head. Mrs. Greene made George go inside, and his brothers and sisters followed behind him. The lemonade turned into sticky puddles all over the sidewalk and street. It was the worst mess I'd ever seen.

Although I hadn't done anything wrong,

I still felt bad. George shouldn't have shoved Tina, but he was right. The lemonade was the worst in the world. Amber, Lydia, Lena, and Lana helped us gather up everything and take it back inside. Then everybody went home.

"I guess you were right about the lemonade. It really did stink," Tina said before we went to sleep that night. "I'm sorry my plan didn't work."

"That's okay, Tina. You did your best," I said.

Soon she was asleep. I lay awake for a while. Except for the ten dollars I'd made today, I still didn't have the cookie money. It was up to me now to come up with my own plan.

STEP #7:
Go to Plan B

My granddad says that when you need to find an answer to a problem, you should sleep on it. Then you'll have the answer when you wake up the next morning. The night after the nasty lemonade sale I decided to take my granddad's advice. Before I went to sleep, I wrote a question on a sheet of paper. The question was:

How should I earn back the cookie money?

I folded up the paper, put it under my

pillow, and slept on it like my granddad said to do. That night I dreamed about Doofus Doolittle.

In my dream, his furry little face was next to mine. He touched my nose with his cold little nose, just the way he does when he wakes me up sometimes.

When my mom called me the next morning for breakfast, I jumped out of bed fast. Then Doofus Doolittle came into my room and rubbed up against my leg. It was like he was reminding me of something. And it was then my dream came back.

I picked him up and gave him a hug. He tilted his head to the side and meowed. Sometimes, I think Doofus is the cutest cat I've ever seen. And then the answer to my problem came to me.

Every kid on our street thought that his

or her pet was the cutest in the world. Lydia and Amber thought Snowflake, their white Persian cat, was the cutest. Booker and Betty have hamsters. They thought they were the cutest. The Greenes have two dogs, goldfish, and two birds. They all thought their pets were the best. The answer to my cookie-money problem was all the cute, smart animals on the block. In other words, a pet show to decide whose pet was *really* the best.

I could call it the Oak Street Pet Show. I would charge each kid on the block a fee to enter his or her pet in the show. I would also charge kids who didn't have pets an admission fee. I would make lots of money. Maybe even more than I needed. Suddenly, I started to feel better.

I pulled on my jeans and my sneakers.

Then I ran downstairs as fast as I could. I could hardly wait to tell Tina about my plan. This was the best idea I'd ever had.

"Morning . . . Willie," Tina said when I sat down. Both my mom and dad were sitting at the table. I figured that was why she didn't call me the usual name. My dad smiled at her approvingly.

"I'm happy you remembered, Tina," he said.

When my parents were gathering their things for work, I told Tina about my idea. She agreed that it was a winner.

I finished breakfast and then went outside to look for Amber. Lena and Lana were playing on her front porch, even though it was still early. When I told them my idea, they agreed that it was a good one.

"Let's make a list," said Amber. The four

of us sat there for a while, trying to figure out what to write. Then I thought about what my mom said reporters ask themselves when they report a story. She said they always ask themselves the five Ws: *Who, What, Where, When,* and *Why.*

So I wrote down the first W—*Who*. I wrote down my name. Willie Thomas. Then I wrote down the Oak Street Association. I liked the way it sounded—official. *What*—a pet show. *When*—tomorrow afternoon. *Where*—the Greenes' yard. I paused for a minute. I'd have to ask the Greenes if it was okay, but I knew they'd say that it was. *Why*—to find the cutest, smartest pet on Oak Street.

I read my list over. Then I wrote down the things to do:

1. Ask Gregory Greene's permission for his backyard.
2. Make and hang signs.
3. Find a judge.
4. Make a plaque for first prize.
5. Get Doofus ready.

The first two steps were easy. I asked Amber, Lena, and Lana to help me collect the signs we'd used for the lemonade sale. We printed new signs about the pet show on the back of the old signs.

Is your pet cute?
Is your pet talented?
Enter your pet in the Oak Street Pet Show.
75¢ Pet Admission
50¢ Without Pet
When: Tomorrow afternoon: 1:30
Where: The Greenes' Backyard

We hung the new signs in the same places we'd hung the signs for the lemonade. I asked Candy, Pauline's babysitter, if she would be the judge. She is always fair and never takes sides. Then I made a first

prize. I took a square piece of wood and covered it with tinfoil. I pasted gold stamps all around it. Then I took a big blue ribbon and attached it to the end. I asked Tina to write in cursive "Cutest, Smartest Pet on Oak Street" on a piece of white paper, and glued it in the middle.

The first four things were crossed off my list. Finally, everything was ready. Everybody on the street was excited. Everybody had brushed, washed, or rehearsed their pet. Everybody was sure his or her pet would win.

The next thing was Doofus Doolittle. The only thing that Doofus Doolittle hates more than the vet is taking a bath. I knew that giving him a bath for the pet show was out of the question. So I decided I would just brush his fur and tie a red ribbon around his neck.

That night I dreamed about Doofus Doolittle in his red ribbon. In my dream, I taught him how to play "Chopsticks" on the piano. I woke up the next morning thinking about how he really was the best pet in the world. Even if he couldn't play a note.

STEP #8:
Okay,
So Have a Plan C

I was so excited about the pet show I almost forgot what day it was. But then I remembered. It was Friday. I only had three more days to earn back the cookie money. I had a lot riding on the pet show.

After breakfast I went outside to get things ready. I found a tin can to put the money in and placed it on the old table in the Greenes' backyard. The table only had three legs, so Gregory helped me balance it with a stack of magazines. Then I sat down behind the table. Because I was running the contest, Tina entered Doofus Doolittle. Her seventy-five cents were the first coins to drop into the tin can. Lana and Lena stood beside Tina.

"I wish we—" started Lena.

"Could have a pet, but Aunt Wynn—" added Lana.

"Doesn't like animals—"

"Not even birds!" Lana said. "So we'll cheer for Doofus—"

"Doolittle!" finished Lena.

Lena took Doofus Doolittle from Tina and hugged him.

Amber and Lydia were next in line. I knew they thought Snowflake, their cat, was going to win. I had to admit that Snowflake was a pretty cat. Lydia brushed her fur until it was fluffy and beautiful. Lydia tied a lacy pink ribbon around Snowflake's neck.

Even so, I didn't think that Snowflake could beat Doofus Doolittle. The prize was for more than just being pretty. It was for personality and talent, too. Snowflake is beautiful, but Doofus Doolittle has a good personality.

"Good luck!" I said to Amber. I wished I had thought of making two first-prize awards.

Betty and Booker were the next kids in line. Betty was carrying her hamsters, Boo and Koo, in their cage. Booker was walking beside her.

"Aren't they cute?" said Betty with a grin.

"I hope Boo and Koo win!" added Booker. I smiled even though I really didn't think they had much of a chance. The only thing they can do is run around on their little wheel and drink water from their bottle. But I knew Betty and Booker would be so disappointed if their pets didn't win the contest. Why hadn't I made enough prizes for everybody?

The Greenes were the next five kids in line. I had promised Gregory that they could enter one of their pets for free because the pet show was going to be in their backyard, so I didn't charge him for Casey, his dog. Casey looks like three dogs rolled into one. He is long and low to the ground like a dachshund. He has a face like a cocker spaniel. He sounds like a German shepherd when he barks, and he can run very fast, even though his legs are short.

George was next in line. He was entering Rusty, an Irish setter. Rusty is fifteen years old, which is nearly one hundred years for people. Mostly he likes to lie in the sun and sleep. I wished I'd thought of making a prize for the oldest dog.

"How much money is the prize?" George asked as he dropped his seventy-five cents into the can.

"It's not money; it's a plaque," I said.

He looked doubtful. "That's not fair! Nobody wants a dumb plaque."

"Money isn't everything!" I said.

"So what kind of plaque is it?" he asked.

"You'll see if you win," I said.

I was starting to get a little worried. When I'd made the prize, I hadn't thought too much about it. What if the winner was disappointed? What if he or she wanted his or her money back? What if people didn't agree with Candy? Maybe the Oak Street Pet Show wasn't such a terrific idea after all.

Grace Greene entered her lovebirds, Mitch and Match, who were sitting in their cage. I felt kind of bad when I took her seventy-five cents. She was sure her birds would win, but I didn't think so. The only thing they could do was coo. I didn't even think they could fly. But Grace really loved them.

Gandy and Goldy, the Greenes' cousins from Detroit, were next in line. They entered their two goldfish, who they named after themselves—Gandy and Goldy. I was afraid they had about as much chance of winning the prize as Mitch and Match did. Why had I only

made one first prize? I asked myself again.

Pauline, who is allergic to fur, was next in line. She was holding a bird in a cage, too. I knew it must be Tweetie, Mrs. Pyle's bird. Tweetie was a canary. He was bright yellow, just like the bird in the cartoon. His cage had a big red bow on top.

"Tweetie is visiting me. Mrs. Pyle is letting me take care of him while she is on vacation," Pauline said. She put the cage on the table because it was heavy. "She'll be so surprised when Tweetie wins the prize!"

"Good luck!" I said cheerfully, even though I didn't feel very cheerful. Everybody, even my next-to-best friend, was going to be disappointed.

Five or six kids who had heard about the pet show from other streets brought their pets, too. One girl brought a tiny kitten. A boy named Leon brought a green snake. Another kid brought a plastic bowl with colorful fish.

Everybody was smiling and happy.

Everybody was sure that his or her pet would win.

I cleared my throat. "Ladies and gentlemen. Welcome to the first annual Oak Street Pet Show," I said in a loud voice. I'd said "annual" because it made it sound official.

"I'd like to introduce our judge, Candy Keene."

"Don't you mean Candy Cane?" George said.

Candy threw him a mean look. It was the first time I'd ever seen Candy give anybody a mean look. George stopped giggling. Candy stood up straight. She's a teenager, but she really looks like a grown-up. Everybody knew she would be fair.

Since Booker and Betty were first in line, Candy judged their pets first.

"Nice pets." She said it fast as if she didn't really believe it.

Betty could tell.

"He has talent, too. Do you want to see Boo's trick?" Betty asked.

"Okay." Candy sounded uncertain.

Betty opened the cage and took out the hamster. "His trick is when he eats. His cheeks grow real big," she said. She puffed out her own cheeks until they were twice as big as they usually are. "Give me the carrot, Booker," she said. Booker gave her a carrot. She put it near Boo's mouth. Boo started to nibble it. He nibbled and nibbled until his cheeks were filled with food.

"That's not a trick; all hamsters and guinea pigs do that," George said. He had come to the front of the line to see what was going on.

Betty ignored him. "Hold Boo for a minute, Candy. Then you'll see how cute he is," she said.

"No! He looks too much like a mouse," Candy said. I could tell by the look on Candy's face that she didn't want to hold Boo.

"But Boo is a *hamster*!" Betty said. She handed Boo to Candy just as Candy threw up her hands. Boo grabbed Candy's blouse with his tiny claws. Candy screamed. Boo slid down the front of Candy's blouse to the ground. Betty screamed. Boo scampered away. He ran as fast as his little legs could carry him.

That was just about the time that my dream about the Oak Street Pet Show turned into a nightmare.

STEP #9:
Don't Even Think About a Plan D!

Doofus Doolittle must have thought that Boo was a mouse, too. The moment he saw Boo run across the yard, Doofus Doolittle jumped out of Tina's arms. He sprang to the ground and took off after Boo.

"Stop, Doofus Doolittle!" Tina screamed.

"Oh, no! Your cat is going to get my hamster! Run, Boo, run!" Betty screamed. Suddenly, Gregory's dog, Casey, broke away from him. He turned in Doofus Doolittle's direction, and off he went.

"Run, Doofus Doolittle! Run!" I screamed.

"Look out, Boo!" Betty yelled. "Don't let him catch you."

Boo ran in a circle. Doofus Doolittle ran behind him. Casey ran after Doofus Doolittle. Then Boo ran under the merry-go-round. Doofus Doolittle ran after him. Casey

stood waiting for them to come out. Boo ran
out and headed under the table. Doofus
Doolittle chased after him. Casey followed
Doofus Doolittle. Betty dove under the table
to rescue Boo. I ducked under the table to
rescue Doofus Doolittle. The table tipped
over. Tweetie's cage fell on the ground.

Tweet! Tweet! Tweetie screeched.

"Oh, no! Oh, no!" screamed Pauline. She ran to pick up the cage just as Snowflake leaped out of Amber's arms. Snowflake landed in a mud puddle near the table. Then she hopped on top of Tweetie's cage and began to rattle it with her paws.

"Snowflake!" Amber screamed as she tried to pry her pet's claws off the cage. Suddenly, Rusty rolled out of his spot in the sun. He started to howl as he strolled toward Snowflake. Snowflake jumped back into the mud and then headed up a tree. Everybody's pet was suddenly barking, howling, meowing, squeaking, or squawking. Betty and Booker began to wail.

Mrs. Greene came running out of the house waving her hands in the air. "What in the world is going on out here?" she yelled.

Doofus Doolittle ran into Mrs. Greene's

garden. Casey chased him. Snowflake screeched and tried to claw her way up the tree. Rusty stood underneath it, howling and growling. Tweetie was flying around his cage trying to get out. Mitch and Match were squawking in theirs.

Mrs. Greene looked around her backyard. It was a mess. The magazines that Gregory had placed under the table leg were spread out on the ground. Torn paper was everywhere.

"I think it's time for everybody to go home!" said Mrs. Greene. She grabbed Rusty by his collar and pulled him from under the tree. "I will be back out here in ten minutes. I want my children in this house and all other children and animals out of my backyard!" she said. Mrs. Greene had never yelled at anyone before.

"What a dumb idea this pet show was!" Gregory said.

"Yeah!" said the kid who had the snake.

"Look what happened to Snowflake!" Amber said as she pulled her kitty out of the tree. Snowflake's pink ribbon was nowhere to be seen, and she was covered with mud.

"We'll have to take her to the vet to get her groomed!" Lydia glared at me.

"Get your dog away from my cat!" Tina yelled at Gregory.

"This is your dumb sister's fault!" Gregory said as he pulled his dog away from Doofus Doolittle.

"Don't call my sister dumb! Shut up before I hit you!" Tina said.

"Dumb! Dumb! Dumb!" Gregory said, looking in my direction.

Tina picked up Doofus Doolittle and left the Greenes' backyard. I wondered if she was mad at me, too.

Pauline picked up Tweetie's cage and dusted it off.

"If Mrs. Pyle finds out about this, she'll never let me watch Tweetie again." She looked like she was going to cry as she left the yard holding Tweetie's cage. Candy just looked at me and sighed. I could tell she felt sorry for me.

"Where is Boo?" Booker asked me. The last time I'd seen Boo was when Doofus Doolittle had chased him under the table.

"I want Boo!" Booker said. Betty started to cry. Lena and Lana were still in the yard, too. They came over and Lena put her arm around Betty.

"We'll help you—"

"Find him," Lana said.

Lena took a carrot and a stalk of celery out of Boo's cage. Then she and Lana spread chunks of carrot and celery everywhere. Then they sat quietly on the ground and waited.

Soon Boo came out. He looked around very slowly. Lena held out a chunk of carrot, and he took it in his paws. Lena carefully picked him up and gave him to Booker.

"Boo!" Betty said very softy. She took him from her brother and gave him a kiss. She put him back in his cage with the other hamster. They left the Greenes' backyard smiling. That made me feel a little bit better.

Lena and Lana walked me home. They were the only kids on the block who were talking to me, the only ones who hadn't had pets in the show. When we got to my house, we sat down on my back porch. I wasn't ready to face anybody yet.

"Cheer up, Willie, it's not your fault," Lena said.

"Yes it is," I said.

"But you were just trying to earn some money," Lana said.

All I could do was sigh.

"We're really sorry," Lena and Lana said, both at the same time. Lena dropped her eyes. Lana dropped hers, too. I had never told them that I'd spent the cookie money on them, but I wondered if they had guessed.

"Can we—" Lena started.

"Do something to help?" Lena finished the sentence she had started.

I thought for a moment. "That's okay," I said. I was glad that they offered to help, but I wasn't up to any other moneymaking ideas. After the lemonade stand and the pet show, I didn't think I could take it.

When I went inside, Mrs. Cotton was setting the table for dinner. I knew my mother and father would be home soon. I went to my room and closed the door. After a while, Tina came in.

"Are you mad at me, too?" I asked. "You can tell me the truth."

"Not mad, just embarrassed that you're my sister," Tina said. I knew I shouldn't have asked. Sometimes Tina didn't know when to stop. "But everybody else on the block is mad at you. Everybody wants their money back. Everybody. Even Lydia and Amber," she added.

"I feel terrible," I said. Tina pulled out the tin can with the money in it. "Want me to give it back for you?" she asked.

"Yeah," I said.

"It was a good idea, Willie. It just didn't work out," she said. "Like the lemonade sale." She put her arm around me then, and we sat there on the bed for a while.

Tina took the tin can and went outside to give everybody back their money. She asked if I wanted to help her, but I told her no. All I wanted to do was just sit there for a while. I couldn't stop thinking about what had happened.

It was all because I was trying to earn some money because I hadn't told th

wouldn't tell anybody their secret. I had broken that promise when I told Tina. I didn't want to do it again, especially not in writing. On the other hand, I didn't want anybody to think that I'd spent all the money on myself. So I wrote:

a very worthy cause.

But a worthy cause could be anything, I realized. So I added:

Someone on my street was hungry, and I bought them lunch for two weeks. I'm very, very sorry that I spent the cookie money. I never should have done it. I will never do it again. Here is ten dollars that my sister and I made selling lemonade. I promise that I will pay the rest back as soon as I can.

And then I added:

Somehow.

There didn't seem much else to say. So I finished my letter:

Sincerely,
Willimena T. Thomas
(Willie)

I read the letter three times to make sure it was okay. It said exactly what I wanted to say. I made two more copies, one for my mom and dad, and one for the Girl Scouts, and put each in an envelope. Monday I would take Mrs. Jones her letter and the one for the Girl Scouts of America. I didn't want to think about what she would say or how she would feel. I just knew I had to face her and tell her the truth. Even if it was in a letter.

I had to face my parents, too. I placed their letter on the bureau in their room. I leaned it up against the mirror so they would see it first thing when they came home. For a moment, I had second thoughts. But then I was happy it was done, even though I was still a little scared about what they would say. I knew they would be mad at me.

Okay, I was wrong about my parents being mad. They were furious with me, even though they said I'd done the right thing in the wrong way. I had to pay back all the money from the savings account my father keeps for me at the bank. It was money I was saving to buy myself a Game Boy. But I felt good about giving the money back. Real good.

Like I figured, I was on punishment for a month, of course, and I couldn't watch TV for two weeks. Two whole weeks! So Tina watched whatever she wanted to watch.

She tried not to gloat, but I know my sister better than anybody else in the world, so she couldn't hide her true feelings from me.

Even though I hadn't told them, my mom and dad guessed who the hungry kids on the block were. My mom stopped by to see Miss Wynn and invited Lena and Lana to spend the night whenever they wanted to. She also told Mrs. Cotton to make enough sandwiches for any kid who wanted to come for lunch at our house—

even if it was the whole block.

Lena and Lana came practically every day after that, which was great for me. There was somebody else to tell Tina how yucky her tuna-fish-and-ketchup sandwiches were. But the best thing is that Lena and Lana won't be hungry anymore, and that made everything that had happened during the terrible week of the cookie money worth going through.

But I wouldn't want to go through it again.

Not ever.

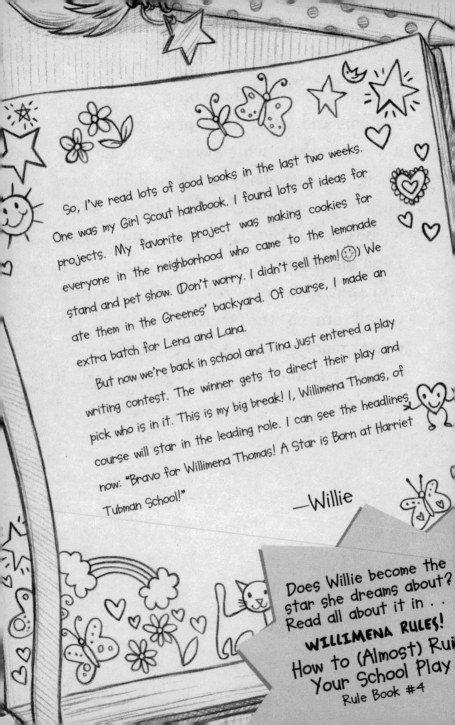

So, I've read lots of good books in the last two weeks. One was my Girl Scout handbook. I found lots of ideas for projects. My favorite project was making cookies for everyone in the neighborhood who came to the lemonade stand and pet show. (Don't worry. I didn't sell them! ☺) We ate them in the Greenes' backyard. Of course, I made an extra batch for Lena and Lana.

But now we're back in school and Tina just entered a play writing contest. The winner gets to direct their play and pick who is in it. This is my big break! I, Willimena Thomas, of course will star in the leading role. I can see the headlines now: "Bravo for Willimena Thomas! A Star is Born at Harriet Tubman School!"

—Willie

Does Willie become the star she dreams about? Read all about it in . . .

WILLIMENA RULES!
How to (Almost) Rui
Your School Play
Rule Book #4